Underground

A Level Two Reader

By Cynthia Klingel and Robert B. Noyed

The Child's World®

Plants and animals live in many different places. One of these places is under the ground.

Underground it is dark and cool. Plants grow above the ground. Their roots grow under the ground.

Roots sometimes provide food for small animals. A few animals even make their homes in or near roots.

Many underground animal homes are in holes called burrows. Tunnels lead to and from the burrows. Some of the tunnels lead to the surface.

Animals live underground for protection. It is easy to hide in these underground homes.

Underground is also a safe place to have babies. Some animals make nests under the ground. They bring grass and leaves from above the ground to line their nests.

Rabbits make their homes underground. So do prairie dogs, gophers, and mice.

Worms also live underground. They eat the soil as they move through it. Worms help keep the soil loose.

Ants live underground, too. They live in large groups called colonies. Like worms, ants tunnel through the soil.

Underground is a hidden world filled with animal life. Living there is very different from living above the ground. It is a special place.

Index

animals, 3, 7, 11, 12, 20

ants, 19

babies, 12

burrows, 8

food, 7

gophers, 15

homes, 7, 8, 11, 15, 19

mice, 15

nests, 12

plants, 3, 4

prairie dogs, 15

protection, 11, 12

rabbits, 15

roots, 4, 7

soil, 16, 19

tunnels, 8, 19

worms, 16, 19

To Find Out More

Books

Dunrea, Olivier. *Deep Down Underground.* New York: Simon & Schuster Children's Books, 1991.

Phinney, Margaret Yatsevitch. *Exploring Underground Habitats.* New York: Mondo Publishing, 1999.

Web Sites

Photo Encyclopedia: Ants
http://ant.edb.miyakyo-u.ac.jp/INTRODUCTION/Gakken79E/Page_02/html
To learn all about the lives of ants.

Underdogs: Prairie Dogs at Home
http://www.nationalgeographic.com/features/98/burrow/index.html
For information about the underground world of prairie dogs.

Note to Parents and Educators

Welcome to The Wonders of Reading™! These books provide text at three different levels for beginning readers to practice and strengthen their reading skills. In addition, the use of nonfiction text gives readers the valuable opportunity to *read to learn*, not just to learn to read.

These leveled readers allow children to choose books at their level of reading confidence and performance. Level One books offer beginning readers simple language, word choice, and sentence structure as well as a word list. Level Two books feature slightly more difficult vocabulary, longer sentences, and longer total text. In the back of each Level Two book are an index and a list of books and Web sites for finding out more information. Level Three books continue to extend word choice and length of text. In the back of each Level Three book are a glossary, an index, and a list of books and Web sites for further research.

State and national standards in reading and language arts emphasize using nonfiction at all levels of reading development. The Wonders of Reading™ books fill the historical void in nonfiction for primary grade readers with the additional benefit of a leveled text.

About the Authors

Cynthia Klingel has worked as a high school English teacher and an elementary teacher. She is currently the curriculum director for a Minnesota school district. Writing children's books is another way for her to continue her passion for sharing the written word with children. Cynthia is a frequent visitor to the children's section of bookstores and enjoys spending time with her many friends, family, and two daughters.

Robert Noyed started his career as a newspaper reporter. Since then, he has worked in communications and public relations for more than fourteen years for a Minnesota school district. He enjoys writing books for children and finds that it brings a different feeling of challenge and accomplishment from other writing projects. He is an avid reader who also enjoys music, theater, traveling, and spending time with his wife, son, and daughter.

Published by The Child's World®, Inc.
PO Box 326
Chanhassen, MN 55317-0326
800-599-READ
www.childsworld.com

Photo Credits
© 2002 David Tipling/Stone: 2
© Dwight Kuhn: cover, 6, 13, 17, 18, 21
© James P. Rowan: 10
© 2002 Laurie Campbell/Stone: 9
© 2002 Mark Katzman/Stone: 5
© 2002 Stephen Krasemann/Stone: 14

Project Coordination: Editorial Directions, Inc.
Photo Research: Alice K. Flanagan

Library of Congress Cataloging-in-Publication Data
Klingel, Cynthia Fitterer.
Underground / by Cynthia Klingel and Robert B. Noyed.
     p. cm.
ISBN 1-56766-975-1 (lib. bdg. : alk. paper)
1. Burrowing animals—Juvenile literature.
2. Underground ecology—Juvenile literature.
[1. Burrowing animals. 2. Underground ecology. 3. Ecology.]
I. Noyed, Robert B. II. Title.
QL756.15 .K55 2001
591.56'48—dc21
                              00-013177

24